CARLOS'S HOME

STUBBS'
CANDY CARNIVAL

SARAH'S HOME

TOM'S
HOME

GRAND CENTRAL STATION
(THE SEARCHER'S CAVE)

CENTRAL
PARK

HUDSON
RIVER

ISLAND
OF THE KIIRBS

For Shaun and Kevin
– AVI

For my parents
– B.F.

Text copyright © 1993 by Avi
Illustrations copyright © Brian Floca
Spanish translation by José Aranda and Anthony Trujillo

This book was originally published in hardcover
by Orchard Books in 1993.

ISBN 978-0-545-54256-2 (hardcover)
ISBN 978-0-545-39880-0 (paperback)

10 9 8 7 6 5 4 3 2 1   13 14 15 16 17

Printed in China 38
This edition first printing, December 2013

City of Light, City of Dark title design by Jeannine Riske
Book design by Phil Falco

The text of this book is hand lettered. The illustrations are
rendered in pen and india ink applied with a brush.

As a boy growing up in New York City, I loved the subways. I liked to stand in the first subway car and watch the train zip through underground passages. I also loved airplanes and had the notion that I might one day build my own. And I loved comic books. *City of Light, City of Dark* contains all of these affections.

On one of my many childhood subway rides, I noticed that on the West Side line, local side, there was an abandoned station at 18th Street. I wondered why it was not used, and what purpose it might serve. I created my own fantastic reason in this book.

In 1991, when Brian Floca and I created *City of Light, City of Dark*, New York City was different. The story happens before 9-11, so those monumental towers, the "Twin Towers," were still standing. You can see them on page 160, in Brian's magnificent illustration.

New York's subway system is much the same today as it was when I was growing up. One exception: Today you must buy an electronic pass — like a credit card — to ride the train. Until 2003, you purchased a token — for $1.25 — that looks exactly as depicted in this book.

Sometimes we think fantasy and adventure are only for old times and distant places. You'll find them here, in one of the great cities of the world — the place I lived. I hope you enjoy *City of Light, City of Dark*. Hopefully it will bring fantasy and adventure to the place you live.

AVI
January 2013

These Kurbs owned an Island as well as the sky above it. And with their POWER they controlled both day and night. For Kurbs have always thrived in darkness, turning to the dark as moths turn to light.

Years ago, when People first came to the Kurbs' Island, they wanted to build themselves a City there. First, however, they had to ask permission of the Kurbs. To this request the Kurbs' leader replied,

PEOPLE! THE LAND YOU WISH TO BUILD ON BELONGS TO US, THE **KURBS.** STILL, WE ARE WILLING TO **LEND** YOU THIS ISLAND AS WELL AS OUR **POWER** SO YOU MAY HAVE THE LIGHT AND WARMTH YOU HUMANS REQUIRE. **BUT THERE IS A PRICE.** EACH YEAR YOU **MUST** ENACT A RITUAL TO SHOW YOU ACKNOWLEDGE THAT THIS ISLAND REMAINS **OURS** AND IS GOVERNED BY **OUR** RULES. IF YOU **FAIL** TO PERFORM THIS RITUAL — BE WARNED! — THE CONSEQUENCES FOR YOU WILL BE **DIRE!**

To this pronouncement the People listened and finally agreed. So the Kurbs established —

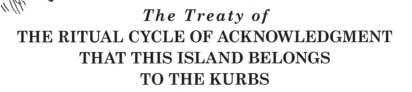

The Treaty of
THE RITUAL CYCLE OF ACKNOWLEDGMENT
THAT THIS ISLAND BELONGS
TO THE KURBS

Wheras:

1) Each year, on the 21st day of June, the Kurbs shall hide their POWER somewhere in some from in the People's City.

2) The People will have six months to search for it.

3) When the People find the POWER, they shall return it to a place of safekeeping, designated by the Kurbs, no later than noon on the 21st day of December.

4) If the POWER is *not* returned, the City will grow so dark and POWER somewhere in some from in the People's City.

5) And the Kurbs will take their Island back.

Furthermore:

6) From the moment the Kurbs hide their POWER on the 21st of June, the hours of City daylight shall begin to decrease.

7) When the POWER is ritually returned to its place of safe-keeping on the 21st of December, City days shall sart to grow warm. The hours of daylight will lengthen.

Finally:

8) THE RITUAL CYCLE OF ACKNOWLEDGMENT marks two halves of the human year, December to June, June to December For the first six months the POWER shall be kept safe in a place designated by the Kurbs. For the second six months the POWER will be hidden somewhere in the city, and the People must search for it. Should the People fail to find the POWER and return it, the Cycle will be broken and the People's lease on this island shall be ended *forever*.

AGREED _____   AGREED _____
For the People   For the Kurbs

Signed on the 45th day of the 13th moon, Kurb year 55122337.

In the early years of this agreement the Kurbs' POWER was hidden in an ear of corn, then a musket ball. Later it was put in an oil lamp. Most recently the POWER has been put within a transit token, the small golden disk used by the People as fare for bus or subway travel.

Who searches for this POWER?

The People chose a woman. She alone had the responsibility of conducting the search. To help her in her searching, the People gave her powers that included special sight.

Now, when this woman had a daughter, the first thing she did was give that girl those powers. Only when the girl was older did her mother provide her with knowledge of the search as well as her future responsibilities. This meant that when the woman died, there was someone new to take up the yearly search. Thus, THE RITUAL CYCLE OF ACKNOWLEDGMENT continued, mother to daughter, mother to daughter, generation after generation.

Now, the means by which the woman passed on her special powers was simple: the POWER — in whatever its form — Was held to the baby's forehead. From that moment the daughter was fated to take on the searcher's responsibilities.

For hundreds of years the cycle of seeking the POWER and of returning it to the safekeeping of the Kurbs continued unbroken. Then, eleven years ago, something very different happened.

In the City there lived a man by the name of Thor Underton. He was a maker of neon signs of every imaginable color — creations brilliant enough to surpass the grandest fireworks, bright enough to turn night into day.

Underton wanted his signs large and built them so. But the larger they grew, the more costly they became to construct and electrify. Indeed, so great was their cost that people began to reject his dazzling designs.

Underton set to work with the assistance of his young apprentice, one Theodore Bitner.

Underton had found Theo abandoned on a dark city street. He took him in, fed and clothed him, and taught him much about sign making and electricity. Naturally, Theo Wished to please Underton.

After much time and many difficulties, Underton — with Theo's help — completed his masterwork — the largest neon sign ever attempted — a gigantic spectacle of sparkling, blazing, blinking, flashing color. Its letters read,

Underton considered atomic power, solar power, sea power, wind power—nothing was enough.

Frantic, he spent hours in libraries. He consulted the Moderns. He studied the Ancients. In so doing he stumbled upon the history of the Kurbs and *their* POWER.

Further research revealed that in recent times this POWER resided in a City transit token.

But would Underton be able to find the one token from among the millions of tokens that existed? He looked for a year but did not find it.

Then he learned that, at that time, the person whose mission it was to search for the token was a young woman named Asterel. He would wait until *she* found the small golden disk. Then, *before* she could restore the token to its place of safekeeping, he would take it and thus gain control of the Kurbs' POWER!

Slyly, Underton confided in Theo about the Kurbs, the POWER, and THE RITUAL CYCLE OF ACKNOWLEDGMENT.

FURTHER

THEO, IF I ASKED YOU TO DO SOMETHING A BIT UNUSUAL, YOU'D BE WILLING TO DO IT, WOULDN'T YOU?

OH, YES, SIR! IT'S THE LEAST I COULD DO.

THEO, THAT SEARCHER OF THE **POWER** I TOLD YOU ABOUT ROAMS THE CITY IN DISGUISE. IN OLDEN TIMES SHE MIGHT HAVE BEEN A MILKMAID OR CHIMNEY SWEEP.

THE ONE WHO HAS THE JOB THESE DAYS, THIS ASTEREL, HAS PRETENDED TO BE A POLICEWOMAN, A BUS DRIVER, A STREET CLEANER.

WHAT IS SHE THIS YEAR?

METER MAID.

THEO, I WANT YOU TO WATCH HER. FOLLOW HER. BEFRIEND HER. AND WHEN SHE FINDS THE TOKEN - AHEM -

TAKE IT.

Theo had no trouble meeting Asterel: he merely parked a car by a fire hydrant. She — a meter maid — gave him a parking ticket. But once the young man and young woman met, they came to like each other. What's more, in the course of time, from January to February, they fell in love.

But the more deeply Theo and Asterel loved, the greater grew their fear that the truth of their identities, if discovered, would split them apart. So they held fast to their secrets — he to the nature of his assignment from Underton, she to her fated mission as the searcher of the POWER.

In the month of March, they married.

Three months after the marriage — at the moment of noon on the 21st of June — Asterel secretly resumed that year's mission of searching for the token hidden by the Kurbs. Theo — just as secretly — spied on her, so he knew when she found the token. But he did not know why his wife slipped off to an underground hideaway beneath the City's Grand Central Station. Though he followed her there, he was unable to see her conceal the token in a hiding place of her own. The truth is, Asterel was to have a baby in December and she needed to keep the token so as to anoint the unborn child. Of that, Theo knew nothing.

In the third week of December, Asterel gave birth to a girl. "Let's name her Estella," she told Theo happily. "The word means 'star.'"

By the morning of the 21st of December, Asterel had regained enough strength to make some excuse to her husband, then slip away to her underground hide-away and fetch the token. With it she intended to anoint her daughter, passing on to Estella the searcher's gift of special sight.

Token in hand to anoint Estella, Asterel returned to the home she shared with Theo. There she found a note:

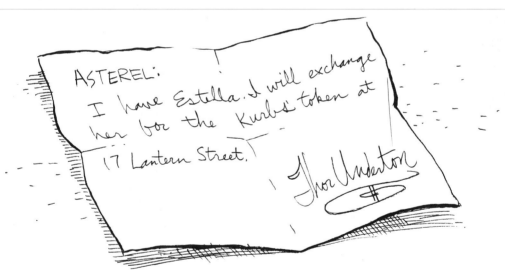

In rage and panic, Asterel raced to Underton's workshop. Instead of bargaining with the genius of light, she commenced to destroy his great sign, shattering the neon tubes into a million slivers of glass. When Underton tried to stop her and save his masterwork, he was accidentally blinded.

Now Asterel faced a terrible decision: should she complete the ritual of the token or set off to search for her baby? She felt she had no choice. She must save the city. In agony she fled the workshop, struggled through the City, and restored the token to its place of safekeeping. Then she fairly flew back to Lantern Street. But Underton, Theo, and her Estella were nowhere to be seen.

That was eleven years ago. In the time since —

Asterel has continued to do as she was meant to do — search for the token and complete the annual ritual. *But she has never stopped looking for her daughter.*

Theo has cared for Estella as lovingly as any father could. But, fearful that Asterel might find him and take their child, he has changed his name, disguised his face, and meekly given over control of his life to Underton. *Above all, he has tried to stay hidden from Asterel.*

As for Underton, he, embittered by blindness, has grown more and more obsessed about the token. Absolutely convinced that its POWER can restore his sight, he devotes all his time, energy, and genius to one goal: *that the token shall be his!*

1ST CHAPTER

THE CITY, THE AFTERNOON OF DECEMBER NINETEENTH.

THE JUAREZ FAMILY — CHILDREN, PARENTS, UNCLES, AUNTS, GRANDPARENTS, AND COUSINS — ARE ALL CHEERFULLY EXHAUSTED FROM EATING TOO MUCH. AMONG THE EXHAUSTED ONES IS CARLOS. HE'S SITTING ALONE NEAR A SLIDING DOOR OVERLOOKING A SMALL BALCONY.

WHAT CARLOS SEES OUTSIDE UPSETS HIM.

FOR THE VIEW CONTAINS EVERYTHING HE HATES ABOUT THE CITY: IT'S BLEAK, UGLY, AND BORING.

AS CARLOS WATCHES, A SCRUFFY SPARROW FLITS THROUGH THE AIR. THE BOY SIGHS. FLYING IS THE WAY HE PLANS TO FLEE THE CITY AND GO HOME, WHERE IT'S WARM AND GREEN.

SOON... SOON.

SAFE WITHIN THE BUILDING, CARLOS CATCHES HIS BREATH. THE BIRDS HAVE TORN HIS SHIRT. HE FEELS BLOOD ON HIS CHEEK.

WHAT MADE THOSE PIGEONS SO FEROCIOUS?

HE LOOKS AT THE DISK HE HAS TAKEN FROM THE DEAD BIRD.

WHAT'S THE BIG DEAL? JUST AN ORDINARY TOKEN.

IS THAT MAN LOOKING FOR ME?

CAN'T BE— HE'S BLIND.

IN THE BEDROOM CARLOS PUTS ON HIS JACKET TO KEEP THE TEARS IN HIS SHIRT FROM BEING SEEN, THEN TURNS UP THE COLLAR TO HIDE HIS SCRATCHES.

HOLA, MAMÁ.

"HI, MOM."

CARLOS! ME TEMO QUE TENEMOS QUE IRNOS PRONTO A CASA.

"CARLOS! I'M AFRAID WE HAVE TO GO HOME SOON."

¿PUEDO MIRAR EL FINAL DE ESTO? ES ACERCA DE LOS PRIMEROS AEROPLANOS.

POR SUPUESTO.

I'LL FLY FARTHER THAN THEY DID.

"CAN I WATCH THE END OF THIS? IT'S ABOUT EARLY AIRPLANES."

"SURE."

MEANWHILE, THE BAG LADY REACHES GRAND CENTRAL STATION....

SIGH...

NOW SHE IS HERSELF AGAIN—
ASTEREL, THE TOKEN SEARCHER.

WHO HAS THE TOKEN?

SHE MAKES A FIST.

IT'S THIS BOY WHO HAS IT.

ONLY THIRTY-SIX HOURS BEFORE THE DEADLINE. IF I DON'T PUT THAT TOKEN WHERE THE KURBS WANT IT, THE CITY WILL FREEZE!

FIND THE BOY! BUT THE CITY HAS MILLIONS OF BOYS. IF I DO FIND HIM, HOW WILL I GET IT FROM HIM? I'M TIRED OF BEING THE ONLY ONE DOING THIS JOB!

I WISH I COULD SEE ESTELLA.

BUT I DON'T KNOW WHAT SHE LOOKS LIKE ANYMORE AND I CAN SEE ONLY PEOPLE I KNOW — OR THE ONE WHO HOLDS THE TOKEN.

YES, I MUST FIND THAT BOY.

IN APARTMENT 7C, 103 110TH STREET...

RECUERDA QUE MAÑANA VOY A JERSEY PARA VER A TÍA NINA QUE ESTÁ ENFERMA. REGRESARÉ EL MIÉRCOLES.

QUISIERA IR CONTIGO. ESTA CIUDAD ES SUCIA Y ME ABURRE.

"NOW REMEMBER, TOMORROW I'M GOING TO JERSEY TO SEE SICK AUNT NINA. BE BACK WEDNESDAY."

"WISH I COULD GO. THIS CITY'S JUST DIRT AND DULLNESS."

LA MAMÁ DE TOM ESPERA QUE VAYAS A QUEDARTE CON ELLOS. TE LLAMARÉ ALLÍ POR LA NOCHE. ¿TIENES DINERO PARA EL AUTOBÚS?

TENGO UNA FICHA. ¿HAS VISTO ESA REVISTA CON UN PLANEADOR DE MANOS?

FIJÁTE QUE NO.

"TOM'S MOTHER IS EXPECTING YOU TO STAY WITH THEM. I'LL CALL YOU THERE TOMORROW NIGHT. YOU HAVE BUS MONEY?"

"A TOKEN. HAVE YOU SEEN THAT MAGAZINE WITH THE HANG GLIDER IN IT?"

"AFRAID NOT."

38

UNDERTON LIVES IN A FORTY-STORY BUILDING AT THE BOTTOM OF THE CITY.

THAT NIGHT THE BLIND MAN CANNOT SLEEP. HE PROWLS THE BUILDING, WANDERING THROUGH EMPTY ROOMS AND DESERTED FLOORS. EVERYWHERE HE GOES, SKOTOS FOLLOWS. FROM TIME TO TIME UNDERTON STOPS AND FACES THE OUTER GLASS WALLS. BEYOND THEM, HE KNOWS, IS THE CITY. THOUSANDS UPON THOUSANDS OF BUILDINGS WITH BRIGHT WINDOWS, LIGHTS TO OUTSHINE THE STARS. UNDERTON SEES NONE OF IT. BUT IN HIS MIND'S EYE HE SEES WHERE CARLOS LIVES. AND SEEING WHERE CARLOS LIVES, HE SEES THE TOKEN.

43

44

45

53

UPSET, SARAH REPLACES THE LITTLE BOOK ON THE SHELF, THEN GOES UPSTAIRS. SHE TAKES THE PHOTO OF THE WOMAN SHE THOUGHT WAS HER MOTHER.

SARAH STARTS HER HOMEWORK, THE PHOTO BEFORE HER. FROM TIME TO TIME SHE GAZES AT IT. "IS THIS REALLY MY MOTHER?" SHE KEEPS ASKING HERSELF.

ON TOM'S ROOF...

57

LO HARÉ. ¿COME SE SIENTE TIÁ NINA?

MEJOR. ¿SABES QUÉ?

MAÑANA TENGO UNA ENTREVISTA AQUÍ PARA UN TRABAJO.

¡FANTÁSTICO! ¡OJALÁ QUE LO GANES!

"I WILL. HOW'S AUNT NINA?"

"FEELING BETTER. GUESS WHAT?"

"I HAVE A JOB INTERVIEW HERE TOMORROW."

"GREAT! HOPE YOU GET IT!"

BUENO, AMOR. ¿VAS A ESTAR BIEN? SÍ.

TE LLAMARÉ A CASA DE TOM.

ADIOS.

"ALL RIGHT, LOVE. YOU GOING TO BE OKAY?"

"YEAH."

"I'LL PHONE YOU TOMORROW AT TOM'S."

"BYE."

BBRING

HELLO?

MAY I SPEAK TO CARLOS JUAREZ, PLEASE?

SPEAKING.

THIS IS SARAH STUBBS, THE ONE WHO ASKED YOU ABOUT THAT TOKEN. I NEED TO TALK TO YOU ABOUT IT.

WHAT FOR?

95

SPONGY AND SHRILL. SHADOW AND SMOKE. PEOPLE SEE THEM ALL THE TIME WITHOUT REALIZING.

WHAT'S UNDERTON HAVE TO DO WITH THEM?

ESTELLA HEARS THE TRUTH ABOUT UNDERTON.

MY FATHER HAS BEEN PAYING HIM MONEY FOR YEARS.

IN RETURN HE PROMISES TO PROTECT YOUR FATHER FROM ME.

WHY?

SARAH LEARNS HOW ASTEREL AND THEO MET, ABOUT THEIR LOVE, MARRIAGE, AND CHILD.

MAYBE MY FATHER DIDN'T KNOW WHERE YOU WERE.

HE CAME TO ME TONIGHT.

BUT WHEN YOU HAD THE TOKEN, COULDN'T YOU SEE ME?

I HAVE THE POWER TO SEE WHO HAS THE TOKEN. TO SEE ANYONE ELSE, I MUST KNOW **EXACTLY** WHAT THEY LOOK LIKE. YOUR FATHER TOOK ON A DISGUISE TO PREVENT MY SEEING HIM.

AS FOR YOU, I LOOKED FOR YOU EVERYWHERE I WENT. BUT THE TWO-DAY-OLD BABY I KNEW NO LONGER EXISTS, DOES SHE?

UNDERTON TOOK CARE NEVER TO COME HERE. THIS MORNING HE DID, AND WHEN I FOLLOWED HIM I SAW YOU FOR THE FIRST TIME.

SARAH STEPS FORWARD. THE SHRIEKS, CRIES, AND SQUEALS OF THE KURBS GROW LOUDER, IN WAVE UPON WAVE OF DEAFENING NOISE. THEN, GRADUALLY, THE NOISE BEGINS TO SUBSIDE UNTIL IT BECOMES A HUM, A MURMUR, THEN— SILENCE.

SOMEONE FROM THE CITY HAS DISCOVERED THE **POWER** OF THE TOKEN. HE'S TRIED HARD TO STEAL IT.

THIS MAN'S NAMED UNDERTON. NOT ONLY DID HE TRY TO STEAL THE TOKEN, HE'S STOLEN MY FATHER AND IS HOLDING HIM HOSTAGE. UNLESS THE TOKEN IS GIVEN TO UNDERTON, HE'LL DESTROY MY FATHER.

OUR TRIBUTE!

OUR TRIBUTE!

OUR TRIBUT

OUR TRIB

TRIBU

I NEED THE TOKEN TO FIND HIM AND SAVE HIM. I PROMISE THAT ONCE HE'S FREE, I'LL BRING IT RIGHT BACK.

PLEASE, I NEED MORE TIME.

RRRRRRRRRRRRRR

RROAR

HOW DARE YOU COME
HERE, CHILD!
THIS PLACE IS FORBIDDEN TO PEOPLE.
YOU TEST OUR ANGER,
AND WE TELL YOU, CHILD, THAT NEVER IN
ALL THE YEARS HAVE WE EXTENDED THE
DEADLINE. NOT BY A DAY. NOT AN HOUR.
NOT ONE SECOND. NEVER.
THE LAND YOU PEOPLE LIVE ON BELONGS TO
US, THE KURBS. IT HAS ONLY BEEN LOANED
TO YOU. IF YOU FAIL TO FULFILL
THE RITUAL CYCLE OF ACKNOWLEDGMENT,
WE WILL TAKE OUR ISLAND BACK. O CHILD,
YOU WHO HAVE THE TOKEN, LISTEN!

THE RITUAL INSISTS THE TOKEN SHALL BE IN ITS REQUIRED PLACE OF SAFEKEEPING BY THE TWENTY-FIRST DAY OF DECEMBER, AT THE STROKE OF NOON, OR YOU PEOPLE SHALL SUFFER THE CONSEQUENCES! THE DEADLINE IS TODAY! **BE WARNED!**

THE TRAIN IS FIVE CARS LONG. SARAH AND CARLOS HAVE TO OPEN AND CLOSE THE DOORS OF EACH CAR BEFORE REACHING THE NEXT. BY THE TIME THEY GET TO THE FRONT CAR, THEY HAVE PASSED STILL ANOTHER STATION.

BY THE TIME THE BOAT
REACHES THE DOCK, A
STORM HAS BEGUN, A
DRIVING, SLEETING STORM
THAT COVERS EVERY
SURFACE OF THE BOAT
WITH A CRUST OF
SLIPPERY ICE.
   THE THREE BARELY
WAIT FOR THE GANG-
PLANK TO BE LET DOWN
BEFORE THEY RUSH
OFF INTO THE STREET.

THE WEATHER WORSENS. WHIRLING SNOW MAKES IT ALL BUT IMPOSSIBLE TO SEE. VICIOUS WINDS CAREEN UP AND DOWN THE STREETS, BUFFETING ALL WHO DARE TO BRAVE THEM. SO DARK IS IT THAT STREET LAMPS HAVE COME ON. LAMPPOSTS RATTLE. HYDRANTS FREEZE. PEOPLE WALK HUNCHED OVER, HOLDING DOWN COATS, TRYING TO INSULATE THEMSELVES FROM THE CUTTING EDGES OF THE WIND.

TRAFFIC IS AT A CRAWL. THE INCESSANT GRINDING OF FROZEN AUTO ENGINES FILLS THE AIR WITH GROANS THAT SET TEETH ON EDGE.

STUBBS, SARAH, AND CARLOS STRUGGLE DOWN INTO THE NEAREST SUBWAY. THEY WAIT FOR A TRAIN. IT IS TOO COLD FOR TALK. BETWEEN THE TRACKS POOLS OF WATER TURN TO ICE.

IN THE SUBWAY RIDERS ARE QUIETER THAN NORMAL, BUT THEY MUTTER ABOUT THE LACK OF HEAT. EVERY BREATH IS CLOUDED WITH COLD. HANDS ARE WRUNG. FEET TAP.

MINUTE BY MINUTE THE COLD DEEPENS.

THE CITY IS FREEZING.

THE LAST CHAPTER

THAT NIGHT... CARLOS, AS HE HAD PROMISED HIS MOTHER, IS AT TOM'S APARTMENT. HE AND TOM HAVE ALREADY DECIDED NOT TO TELL THE ADULTS WHAT HAPPENED, BECAUSE THEY ARE CERTAIN NO GROWN-UP WOULD BELIEVE IT.

AFTER DINNER, CARLOS'S MOTHER CALLS.

¿ADIVINA QUE PASÓ?

NO PUEDO.

"GUESS WHAT'S HAPPENED?"

"CAN'T."

ME OFRECIERON EL TRABAJO AQUÍ.

¿EN EL CAMPO?

EXACTAMENTE LO QUE QUIERES.

BUENO, MAMÁ, NO ESTOY MUY SEGURO QUE QUIERO IR.

¡CARLOS! ¿QUE HA PASADO CONTIGO?

ESTAN PASANDO COSAS INTERESANTES.

"I GOT A JOB OFFER OUT HERE."

"IN THE COUNTRY?"

"JUST WHAT YOU WANTED."

"YEAH, WELL, MA, I'M NOT SO SURE I WANT TO GO."

"CARLOS! WHAT'S COME OVER YOU?"

"THERE'S SOME INTERESTING STUFF GOING ON...."